T0132045

THE Grandma Quilt

Written by

Susan Hamann

Illustrated by

Jane Oulton and Shirley Monroe

Copyright © 2022 Susan Hamann.

All rights reserved. No part of this book may be used or reproduced by any means, graphic, electronic, or mechanical, including photocopying, recording, taping or by any information storage retrieval system without the written permission of the author except in the case of brief quotations embodied in critical articles and reviews.

Balboa Press books may be ordered through booksellers or by contacting:

Balboa Press
A Division of Hay House
1663 Liberty Drive
Bloomington, IN 47403
www.balboapress.com
844-682-1282

Because of the dynamic nature of the Internet, any web addresses or links contained in this book may have changed since publication and may no longer be valid. The views expressed in this work are solely those of the author and do not necessarily reflect the views of the publisher, and the publisher hereby disclaims any responsibility for them.

Any people depicted in stock imagery provided by Getty Images are models, and such images are being used for illustrative purposes only. Certain stock imagery © Getty Images.

Interior Image Credit: Susan Hamann

ISBN: 979-8-7652-3340-5 (sc)
ISBN: 979-8-7652-3341-2 (e)

Library of Congress Control Number: 2022915508

Print information available on the last page.

Balboa Press rev. date: 08/23/2022

Ryan was 6 – well, almost. Tomorrow was his birthday. But it didn't feel like his birthday. His Gaw wouldn't be here. Gaw was his special name for his grandmother. Every year she had been here for his party, but not this year.

2

Ryan looked out of the window. There was a big brown truck in the driveway. A man got out of the truck with a big box. He walked up the sidewalk to the porch.

"Ryan?" called his mother. "Look at this. It's a package for you. It's from Gaw. What could it be?"

Gaw often sent him cookies but the box was way too big for cookies.

Sometimes she sent him books or puzzles. But it was not the right shape for books or puzzles.

Once it was a picture of the beach. On his birthday that year they went to the beach. This package was too tall and squishy for a picture.

Ryan tore off the brown paper. Inside was a box wrapped in yellow birthday paper. The box felt full to the top but it wasn't very heavy.

He smelled the box. It didn't smell like cookies.

He shook the box but it didn't rattle like books or puzzles.

It didn't have sharp edges like the frame on the beach picture.

Slowly, Ryan untied the ribbon.

Then he took off the yellow paper.

He lifted the lid off the box.

Inside the box was a big folded blanket of many colors.

Ryan looked puzzled. Why would Gaw send him a blanket? He wasn't a baby.

His mother helped him take it out of the box. They spread it out on the floor.

Oh, look, Ryan!" said his mother. "Look what Gaw has made for you. It's a memory quilt – full of all the things you did together."

And it REALLY was. There on the quilt were the things he and Gaw liked best.

A dark blue square had stars and the moon on it. Gaw lived in the country. They would go outside before bed to count the stars. She helped him make a wish on the very first one they saw each night.

The yellow square had three crayons: a red one, a blue one and a yellow one. It was fun to color with Gaw. She once colored a horse blue just because she could.

There was a pale blue square with a red sand pail and shovel. He remembered the birthday they went to the beach. They dug for little clams. The clams kept disappearing but he still brought home the shells they found in the sand.

He Loved
Penguins!

14

Next there was a white square with a black and white penguin wearing a red and green scarf . He loved penguins, especially the stuffed one Gaw had given him when he was a baby.

In one corner was a square with a picture of ice skates. Ryan shivered when he looked at them. One Christmas, when he was very little, they had gone skating on her pond. Gaw held him very tightly because the ice was slippery. It was a scary kind of fun. Gaw kept him safe. Afterward there was hot cocoa and cookies.

Another square had a cat drinking milk from a saucer. That was the story they read at bedtime – a story about a cat who thought the moon was a big saucer of milk. Ryan laughed when he saw the cat.

Gaw's swimming pool was on another square. There were the little waves and the toy boat the sailed back and forth to each other when he was learning to swim.

The next square had a tomato plant with tiny red tomatoes on it. Ryan remembered going to the garden to help pick the little tomatoes. They tasted warm and sweet from the sun.

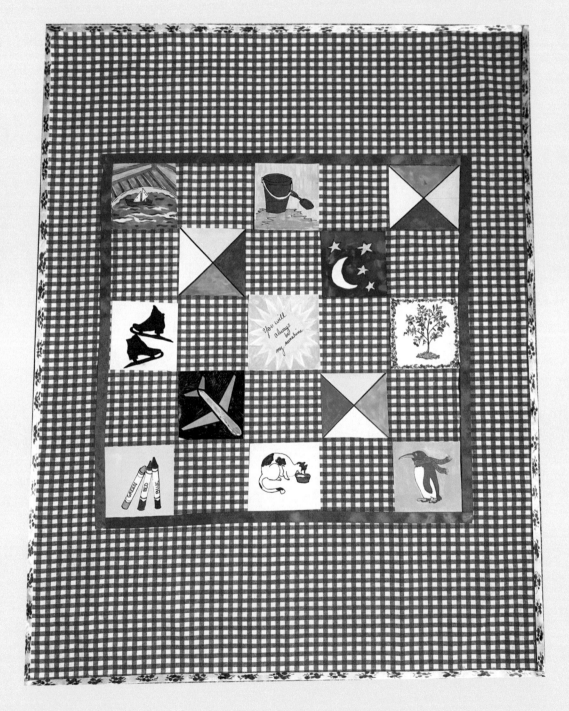

18

There were raspberries sewn around the border of that square. They would pick the raspberries behind the garage to put on their cereal – but usually they ate them before they got back to the house.

A big silver airplane was sewn on a black square. Gaw and he had taken a plane ride to Florida two years ago for his birthday.

And look! Beside it was a square with Mickey Mouse on it. The plane had flown them to see Mickey and all of Mickey's friends at Disney World.

Right in the center of the big quilt was a piece cut out of his favorite blanket from Gaw's big bed. On it was sewn a bright yellow sun and the words "You will always be my sunshine."

Ryan gathered the quilt onto his lap. He wrapped the colors, the pictures, and the memories around him. Now he knew that Gaw would always be there with him – EVERYDAY.

Printed in the United States
by Baker & Taylor Publisher Services